Dr Gilbertson

SIMON AND SCHUSTER

Dr Gilbertson
The Clinic
Garner Bridge
Greendale

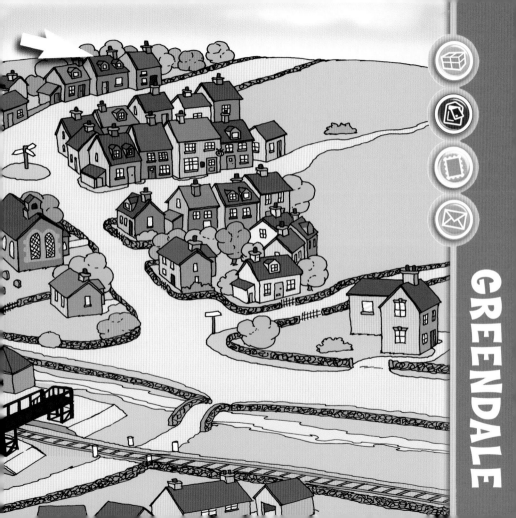

GREENDALE

Come and say hello to Dr Gilbertson!

If any of the villagers in Greendale are feeling unwell, they know their kind doctor will help them get better. Sylvia Gilbertson spends so much time looking after her patients, she can sometimes forget to look after herself...

"Hello there!" a voice called out, as a very swish vintage sports car glided past Pat and Jess.

Pat smiled. He'd know Dr Gilbertson's car anywhere.

"Mum's just dropping me off at school," smiled Sarah, stepping onto the pavement.

"Morning!" said Pat. "Have you got a busy day, Sylvia?"

"I'm all over Greendale today," nodded the doctor. "Lots of poorly people to see."

"Hello, Dr Gilbertson!"

Bill Thompson jogged over to the group. "My mum asked if you could pop in on Dad today. He's got a sore ankle."

"Righto," said the doctor.

Miaow! Jess tugged at Pat's postbag.

"I nearly forgot," said Pat. "Ted Glen looked very under the weather this morning when I gave him his post."

"I'll add him to my list. Bye all!"

Dr Gilbertson visited Ted first.

Ted was huddled inside, warming his feet in a bucket of water. "I dot a dinking cold, Doctor."

"Don't worry, I know just what to do!" Dr Gilbertson announced, quickly taking his temperature.

She gave Ted a drink of honey and lemon and put a blanket round his shoulders.

"Now stay in the warm, for today at least."

Once Ted was feeling a bit better, the doctor got back in her car.

"Bye, Ted! I'm off to see little Nikhil Bains next!" she waved.

"Be careful driving all over Greendale with that roof down," called Ted. "You don't want to catch my cold!"

Dr Gilbertson laughed and started the engine. The wind was a little bracing...

It was time for Baby Nikhil to have his injections.

"Thanks for coming round," said Nisha. "He felt a bit scared at the clinic."

"It's all part of the job," smiled Dr Gilbertson.

The injection was over in no time. The doctor gave Nikhil a special sticker for being so brave.

"See you soon. If he has any problems phone me, night or day."

It was getting quite chilly by the time Dr Gilbertson pulled up at Thompson Ground.

"Can you believe I tripped over a hay bale," grinned Alf.

"Luckily it's only a sprain," said Dr Gilbertson, pulling a stretchy bandage out of her medicine bag.

"Time for a cup of tea, Sylvia?" asked Dorothy.

"Atchoo!" sneezed the doctor. "Sorry no, I've got to pick Sarah up from school."

By the time Dr Gilbertson joined the other mums and dads waiting in the playground, she didn't feel so good.

"Are you shivering, Sylvia?" asked Pat.

She nodded. "I th-think I've p-p-icked up a ch-chill."

"You need to get home, Doctor," said Nisha.

"D-don't worry about m-me," smiled Dr Gilbertson weakly, feeling a lot less brave inside.

"You should see a doctor, Mum," said Sarah.

"I am a doctor!" whispered Dr Gilbertson. "I just need an early night."

Knock knock!

"I'll get it!" she volunteered bravely. "Might be a patient."

Sarah shook her head as Dr Gilbertson went to the front door.

SURPRISE!

Half of Greendale was standing on Dr Gilbertson's doorstep!

"We're here to look after you tonight!" explained Pat.

"I've made fresh soup," said Nisha Bains.

"And I've brought hot water bottles!" added Dorothy Thompson.

"You've looked after all of us so well," smiled Pat. "Now it's our turn to return the favour."

Dr Gilbertson sniffed happily. "With friends like you, I'll be better in no time!"

SIMON AND SCHUSTER

First published in 2006 in Great Britain by Simon & Schuster UK Ltd.
Africa House, 64-78 Kingsway, London WC2B 6AH
A CBS COMPANY

Postman Pat® © 2006 Woodland Animations, a division of Entertainment Rights PLC.
Licensed by Entertainment Rights PLC
Original writer John Cunliffe
From the original television design by Ivor Wood
Royal Mail and Post Office imagery is used by kind permission of Royal Mail Group plc
All Rights Reserved

Text by Mandy Archer © 2006 Simon & Schuster UK Ltd
Illustrations by Baz Rowell © 2006 Simon & Schuster UK Ltd

ISBN 1416910581
EAN 9781416910589
Printed in China